T0380221

Pierre the Poodle Prince & The Lost Isle of Doglantis

Mary L. Boynton

Archway Publishing books may be ordered through booksellers or by contacting:

Archway Publishing
1663 Liberty Drive
Bloomington, IN 47403
www.archwaypublishing.com
844-669-3957

Because of the dynamic nature of the Internet, any web addresses or links contained in this book may have changed since publication and may no longer be valid. The views expressed in this work are solely those of the author and do not necessarily reflect the views of the publisher, and the publisher hereby disclaims any responsibility for them.

Any people depicted in stock imagery provided by Getty Images are models, and such images are being used for illustrative purposes only.
Certain stock imagery © Getty Images.

ISBN: 978-1-6657-5401-9 (sc)
ISBN: 978-1-6657-5403-3 (hc)
ISBN: 978-1-6657-5402-6 (e)

Library of Congress Control Number: 2023923131

Print information available on the last page.

Archway Publishing rev. date: 11/26/2024

PIERRE

&
POODLE PRINCE

AND THE
LOST ISLE
OF
DOGLANTIS

Contents

To The Reader

Please treat this cozy doggerel,
In the spirit that it is written.

For with dogs of all shapes and sizes,
We are surely smitten.

Undying devotion to treats and treasure,
Stretches their talents to full measure.

So, join our Poodle Prince, and his intrepid friends,
In their quest with an agreeably fortuitous end.

Story illustrations are compliments of the author's great-nieces and great-nephews:

Evelyn Hess, Lolo Hess, James Hess and Will Maguire – dog enthusiasts all!

Canine portraits are by Simone Thode.

Cast of Characters

Pierre: White Standard Poodle. Though he bears a royal title, he is truly a dog for all seasons. Pierre is his name; adventure is his game!
Favorite Toy: Blue Monkey
Hobbies: Moonlight bunny hunting with neighbor Taylor and his Cav-King Charles Terrier, Katie. Taylor's Panther-Vision cap helps shine a light on the ever-elusive moon bunnies.

Cooper: Golden Labrador Retriever. He is without a doubt a canine savant and gourmand extraordinaire. "Keyed in the rhythm," he has never met a time that isn't groovy.
Favorite Toy: Hedgehog
Hobbies: If he's not chowing down or snoozing, you can find him playing ball with nonstop delight.

Summer: Golden Retriever. She is at once, ditzy and deep. A charming friend to all.
Favorite Toy: Mr. Carrot, so loved that he has been triple-taped, re-stuffed and is still going strong.
Hobbies: Dog paddling around in her backyard pool with her BFFs.

Olivia: Saint Bernard. A giant of a dog, she is wonderfully imaginative and can be counted on to follow through on commitments. Olivia spends half of each year in majestic Wyoming where she frolics and tumbles in the snow.

Cappy: Long-haired Dachshund. Short in stature, but long on enthusiasm, this darling dachshund lives in San Diego, CA with his best friend Prim, a Corgi mix. They belong to Betsy and Johnny, great friends of the author. Cappy loves to ham it up and is truly coo coo for coconut.

Drago: Irish Wolfhound. Drago is the only character that does not exist in the real world, only in the imagination of the author. He is physically large and naturally intimidating. The historical motto of his breed is "gentle when stroked, fierce when provoked."

Pierre

Cooper

Summer

Olvia

Chapter 1

· ·

It was a dark and stormy night at Dog Park 3. Most of the owners had gathered their canines and called it an evening, hoping to avoid the brewing summer storm. Kathy and a few friends lingered, simply because their dogs couldn't get enough of cavorting and faux-fighting together. They wore each other out and flopped down on the soft grass at the bottom of the hill.

Pierre was first to speak. "Do you think there is any more to life than good food, good friends, and a comfy dog bed?" "This is the dog's life, isn't it?" sighed Summer in agreement. Licking his chops, Cooper chimed in, "Naturally, I think treat time should be all the time! What about you, Olivia?" "Well," she said rolling over on her back, paws akimbo, "I have one of those cute little kegs in my toy basket, and I've always wanted to fill it with treasure. Then I could prance around the neighborhood with the keg around my neck like, you know, the St. Bernards of old." "Cool," said Pierre who loved Olivia's boundless imagination.

"I've heard of a fabulous treasure that could be right under our very paws," panted Cooper. All of the dogs sat stock still, ears at maximum attention. This was shaping up to be a story only Cooper could tell.

Just then an untimely interruption occurred. "Summer, time to go home girl!" Karen smacked her lips in a kiss-kiss. The four dogs whimpered loudly at the same time. Kathy laughed and suggested the dogs get a few more minutes together. "Okay Pierre, ten minutes more. That's it."

"Tell us about the treasure, Coop!" Pierre woofed. Cooper grabbed a nice stick and headed to the scab patch on the far side of the park, with Pierre, Summer, and Olivia nipping at his heels. He stopped and arranged the stick to act like a pencil in his mouth. He then drew what looked amazingly like a dog biscuit. Pierre asked incredulously, "Is this your idea of a treasure, Coop? A biscuit made of dirt?"

"Not at all," chided Cooper. "This is a picture of The Lost Isle of Doglantis. Millions, maybe billions of years ago, this island was situated in the Pacific Ocean. Rumors abound of a fantastic treasure buried on Doglantis by a colony of Poochasaurus, advanced beyond their dog years. Famous *pawleotologist* Sir Rupert Digsalot speculates that hidden beneath the rubble and sand, a fully intact puppy mart exists filled with treats and toys unimaginable."

"We needn't worry about the freshness of said treats, as the Poochasaurus were the first to develop preservation techniques, which they graciously passed down to the Egyptians. I wouldn't be at all surprised if the beef jerky is as if cured last week, and the dog biscuits less petrified than the ones we chew on today," Cooper assured them.

"But what's that got to do with us? We live in the desert," Summer pointed out. Olivia piped in, "Let him finish. I might get to fill my keg after all."

Cooper continued, "Now back to Doglantis. I know a little about geology, and as I recall, all of the land on our planet sits on massive plates that move around over time. When they crash into each other, mountains rise up, when they move sideways continents can actually move or break apart. It is beyond extraordinary. Think of it like the earth sitting on giant dog bowls that move just like yours do Pierre, when you lick the sides. And sometimes the food bowl crashes into the water bowl, making a big mess. But it takes millions of years for any land to move like that."

Cooper's bewildered audience may have been in over their heads, but they were definitely intrigued and wanted to hear more. "The Isle of Doglantis inched its way towards the California coastline until it fit perfectly into the notch of missing land, just like a puzzle piece. Bingo! Doglantis is now part of the desert landscape," Cooper concluded. "Wow!" they chuffed in amazement.

Pierre covered his mop on top with his left paw and panted, "Doglantis, its shape does look awfully familiar. I think I saw something like it at the golf course across the street. Kathy took me there once, but I was asked to leave for lifting my leg on the flagpole at the 18th hole." "How gauche Pierre", exclaimed Olivia. "What in the world does that have to do with Doglantis?" asked Summer. "Well," said Pierre, "there is a big sandy spot, perfect for digging up a storm, and it is shaped like a biscuit, just like Doglantis."

Suddenly all four owners called all four dogs at the same time. "We are going home," they cried in unison.

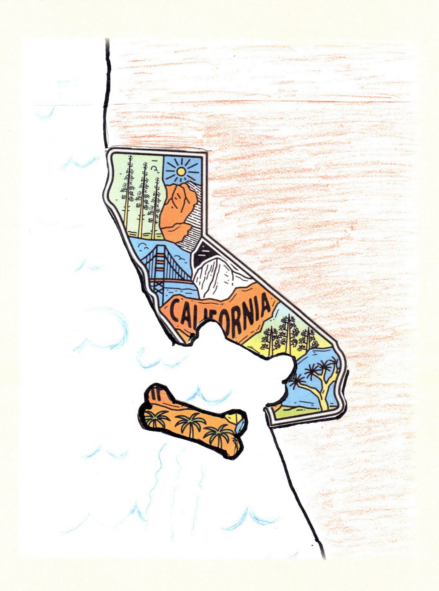

Chapter 2

. . . .

That night, Pierre sped into the house, making a beeline for the kitchen and his water bowl. He lapped with relish until he spilled almost as much as he drank. But little did he care, thoughts of great treasure swirled in the air. What if Cooper is right, and underneath that patch of sand at Duffer Valley Golf Course lay the mother lode of chew toys, frisbees, tennis balls and such? What if a biscuit-shaped island sailing on dog bowls, parking itself on the California coast isn't a completely fantastical absurdity? It seemed to Pierre that he and his pals were long on dreams, and short on plans. A treasure map would certainly be useful.

Kathy was in the den watching Brahma bull riding with the French doors shut tight, so Pierre wouldn't bark his head off at the screen. No one knew why this bovine display provoked Pierre, but it gave him an opening to scour Kathy's purse for a Duffer Valley scorecard displaying a map of the golf course on the flip side. Grabbing the leather handles in his teeth, he gingerly slipped the bag off its perch on the kitchen table onto his corduroy dog bed beneath. Amazed at his own stealth, he tore into the contents, scattering them across the floor. He nuzzled his long poodle nose into the far reaches of her bag and discovered a dog-eared card. Scarcely believing his luck, he stood staring at the closest thing he could get to a treasure map, and there at the 18th hole, he beheld that dreamy, biscuit-shaped patch of sand, known to golfers as a sand trap. Panting gleefully, he used his nose to slide the card under his dog bed. Just as he was about to saunter far away from the scene of the crime, Kathy burst out of the den, saw the mess, and hollered "Pierre, you naughty, unprincely dog! Why is my purse and all of my stuff strewn on your dog bed? Huh? You better not have chewed on those leather straps." As is the lot of dogs, he could say nothing in his own defense. Looking rather sheepish and licking her leg was the only apology he knew.

"Go to bed, Pierre, I'm turning out the lights, and we're turning in." Pierre's head was still spinning from the novel events of the night, but he was legitimately dog-tired and fell right to sleep. The next thing he knew, an eerie specter appeared before him. It was Drago, an Irish Wolfhound from Dog Park 1, disguised as the infamous pirate Captain Henry Morgan. The moustached Drago with canines gleaming, unsheathed a long sword. And raising it over his head shouted menacingly, "DO NOT SEEK THE TREASURE! DO NOT SEEK THE TREASURE!"

Pierre awoke, whimpering, legs twitching. The image of Drago in pirate garb was etched on his brain, and the nightmare message about seeking the treasure played over and over. He had to wonder if that monster-dog overheard Cooper's account of the Doglantis treasure and had designs on it himself.

For all Pierre knew, Drago and his band of big bully-dogs were already scheming to beat Pierre and pals to the booty.

If only morning would come! He climbed up on the bed and nuzzled close to Kathy. Feeling snug and cozy, he fell back to sleep, and didn't stir again until morning.

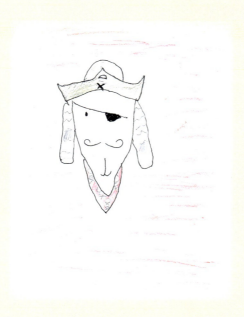

Chapter 3

· ·

Pierre opened his eyes to the glorious desert sun streaming through the plantation shutters. He shook his head and his whole fuzzy body until he felt more alive than ever. Kathy was busy pouring her first cuppa java into a panda mug as Pierre pranced into the kitchen. Morning greetings were always the best, so many hugs and doggy kisses, so much tail-wagging and face-licking. That is what best friends do!

He nudged his bowl, hoping to discover some savory morsels hidden beneath the kibble. "Nope, nothing yet." Pierre took a quick drink of water and made his way to the sliding glass door. Once outside, he began plotting his escape from the yard, calculating how long, in dog minutes, it would take to race over to Dog Park 3, bury the scorecard/treasure map, and high-tail it home before Kathy returned from her line-dancing class. He figured that if he took a tall drink of water, and ran like a greyhound, he might just make it back in time. Kathy took off and not two minutes later, so did Pierre. The Big Dig hinged on his success at camouflaging the map, while keeping it at-the-ready for the madcap planning session tonight.

Did he succeed? Handily! A Sirocco could not have caught up with him, as he skidded under the gate, and halted on their backyard patio, panting furiously. Content that the map was safely sequestered under the chain link fence at DP3, he plopped down in the shade and fell fast asleep.

Pierre awoke to the sound of the SUV pulling into their driveway. He was so excited about the dog park rendezvous that he could scarcely control himself.

He paced, he cried, he dragged out every toy, he whimpered until he got a treat – all in an attempt to make the clock tick faster. All day long, he napped, he roamed, he cased the kitchen for crumbs; he even barked at imaginary intruders on the front lawn.

Kathy couldn't understand what so unsettled her dog, but determined to calm him, she placed Blue Monkey on his dog bed, hoping Pierre would snuggle his favorite toy and fall asleep. Blue Monkey was the only toy that maintained most of its original features, and all of his shaggy limbs. He was indeed Pierre's most valued stuffed friend.

Pierre napped fitfully and was once again visited by that brutish Irish Wolfhound, Drago. This time he traded his barbarous attire for a miner's hat with a nifty flashlight attached, and a snout-nosed shovel was clenched in his teeth. He was trotting resolutely past the dogleg on the 17th hole, squarely towards the seat of the prize on the 18th. Pierre growled and leapt to his feet. They must seek the treasure tonight, if they mean to keep it.

He scarfed down his dinner, barely aware of the teriyaki chicken atop his kibble. He then waited breathlessly as Kathy grabbed his leash and her keys. Pierre was out of the door like a shot. Dauntless and mission-driven, he was dog park bound.

Chapter 4

· · · · · · · · · · · · · · · · · · · ·

Olivia and Summer were already there, racing through the sprinklers on the south-side of the lawn, rewarding all spectators with beads of water bouncing off their shaken fur. Screams and peals of laughter sent the two into a frenzy of sprinkler-chasing and people-soaking. Pierre leapt out of their SUV, anxious to join in.

By the time Cooper arrived, the shenanigans had ceased. The dogs were rolling and pushing against the grass to dry off. They trotted to the fence with Pierre bounding ahead. Pawing and sifting through the dirt, he uncovered the treasure map and signaled for his friends to lie down. Like points on a compass, the four dogs sprawled in four directions, nose to nose to nose to nose! With a note of disquiet, Summer said, "This isn't much of a treasure map. It's awfully small…and dirty." "It'll do" cried Pierre, not a little miffed (given his heroic effort at obtaining it at all). "We all know where Duffer Valley Golf Course is, right? The main thing is that once we get there, we run straight to the 17th hole, just here," said Pierre putting his nose to the map.

"Ah, yes!" cried Cooper, who seemed to understand much with little explanation. "Then we sashay around the dogleg on the 17th, and run right into the Doglantis treasure, just here." Cooper slapped his paw on the sand trap/dog biscuit on the 18th hole.

Olivia raised her giant St. Bernard head, and nodding in agreement, said: "It all sounds doable enough. When do we dig?" "Tonight!" barked Pierre a bit too loudly. In a muted voice he explained: "See that great, black hound across the fence? Well, his name is Drago; I have reason to believe he's caught wind of our caper and is planning to beat us to the treasure."

"He doesn't look like such a bad boy," teased Summer as she tilted her golden head cutely in salutation. "He is trouble enough," declared Pierre. "Twice he has shown up in my dreams, intent on beating us to the punch."

Summer rolled over and shook her shiny coat, "What if I get lost on the way to the golf course? After all, I live furthest away." Cooper grinned, "Happy to be of service! There is one star in the night sky that is brighter than all others. People know it as Sirius, but her more accurate moniker is Dog Star, queen of the Canis Major Constellation. If you keep her above and in front of your nose, she will guide you there, Summer." "Perfect!" she cried.

Olivia also needed reassurance, "Once we get there and dig up the treasure, have any of you geniuses considered how we get home with the considerable loot?" She laid bare a major defect in their otherwise cracker jack plan. They could only carry what they could fit in their mouths. A dogged silence lay like a wet blanket over the droopy group. "I've got it!" cried Olivia. "I'll borrow Denise's golf cart, and we can load it up to its pink canopy with treasure!"

Pierre rolled over and howled with laughter, "Drive a golf cart, hee-hee, that's a good one, Olivia." Cooper and Summer joined in the howl-fest, but Olivia was unabashed. "Seriously, I have watched Denise drive that thing hundreds of times, and before it moves, she puts her foot on a pedal shaped like a bare foot, and the cart rolls forward. If I put both front paws on the pedal, I'm pretty sure I can make it go."

"Then how do you possibly steer?" asked Summer. "Cooper could do it for me. He lives just next door, and the cart is in the driveway between our houses," answered Olivia satisfactorily. "Why not?" Coop replied, "I've had some powerful napping dreams about being a pilot. I'm in."

Pierre was convinced that they were drifting, yet again, into the realm of fantastical absurdity. But little did he care, thoughts of great treasure swirled in the air! Plotting and planning the dig of the century with such affable friends was just too much fun to pooh-pooh.

Pierre sealed the deal, insisting that the four quixotes put their right paws on the map, and swear to go to whatever lengths to seek and secure the treasure. "We reconnoiter at the 17th hole, under the coconut palm at 11 p.m. tonight," declared Pierre. All barked in passionate agreement.

It is notable that the subject of escaping from home without their owners' knowledge or consent was never discussed. Suffice to say dogs are notoriously canny, if not downright sneaky when they need to be. These four are no exception.

So, climbing into our literary vehicle, known as suspension of disbelief, we can safely park ourselves at the edge of Duffer Valley Golf Course, anticipating the arrival of our furry friends.

Chapter 5

. . . .

"**O**OCHI-WA-WA!" yelped Pierre as he screeched to a halt in front of the coconut palm. "Did you say you saw a Chihuahua?" asked Summer trotting up beside him. "Ho-Ho, no. I thought I stepped on a cactus needle, but it's a sharp little peg. I'm alright," he replied. "Okay, but I swear I saw the outline of a small creature over there by the wildflowers," Summer persisted. She was spot-on, for hiding behind a lovely clump of lupines lurked a little doggy of black and brown markings.

"You there, what are you up to? Spying on us? Hoping to horn in on our treasure? Show yourself, little fella!" Pierre regarded interrogation necessary considering the sensitive nature of the Doglantis treasure. A Longhaired Dachshund stepped out of the shadows saying, "I know nothing of spy craft nor treasure. I was snoozing on the front porch and heard the word coconut waft through the air. Once you've lapped up spilled coconut milk, you will forever be a slave to it, so I hurried over to investigate," he explained. Summer replied, "You see, we are meeting under a coconut palm tree, there is no milk." The disappointed doggy turned to go. "Hold on, what is your name? How come we've never seen you at the dog park?" asked Pierre suspiciously.

"My name is Captain, but my friends call me Cappy. I'm just visiting from San Diego, staying with my short-haired cousin, who lives over there, across the road. Might I join you? I promise not to nose in on your prize, but a treasure hunt by moonlight sounds delicious," said Cappy.

"We could use a lookout to warn against intruders; you seem alert and reliable," surmised Pierre. Cappy answered enthusiastically, "On long walks by San Diego Bay, I've listened to many a naval officer discussing the evening's dog watch, I'd be honored to oblige." Pierre explained, "We'll head out as soon as our partners arrive."

No sooner had Pierre finished than a pink golf cart came careening across the grass en route to a collision with the now infamous coconut palm. "Cut the power, Olivia, paws off the pedal before we crash!" yelped Cooper. He waved to his pals, delivering a goofy grin as he jumped out of the cart. Olivia tumbled after.

Pierre and Summer rushed the cart, wagging their tails in furious delight. The circus atmosphere left Cappy astonished and just doggone tickled to be there. Cooper and Olivia approved of the little out-of-towner, and a scherzo of cajoling commenced.

Pierre was all business, "Okay everyone, hop in the cart. Let's hightail it over to the 17th hole. Don't forget Coop, take a right at the dogleg, and head straight towards that luscious dog biscuit near the green, where the flag says 18!" Off they sped into the dark verdancy of the golf course, into the adventure of a lifetime. They reached the sand trap/dog biscuit just as Olivia's achy paws surrendered and slipped from the pedal. No sooner had they exited the cart, than their pint-sized lookout glimpsed a faint beam of light off to the east. It seemed to be heading their way at a rapid clip. "Hey, I think someone is coming!" said Cappy in a raspy voice.

"Unbelievable!" huffed Pierre. "It's Drago, the Scourge of Dog Parkdom come to steal our treasure, Grrrr!" Pierre and Cooper rushed the interlopers. Summer sensed a scuffle about to ensue, so she jumped between the opposing teams. And in her sincerely ingenuous and endearing voice said, "Boys, don't you suppose the Doglantis treasure is big enough for all of us? Think about it Pierre, Drago was sensible enough to bring along a flashlight, so we can actually see what we find." Olivia added, "Yes, and with all of those paws digging, we can fill up the cart much faster."

Drago was captivated by Summer's charm and vowed in the moment to make peace with Pierre and Cooper, if he could just dig alongside her. As challenge left Drago, a spirit of cooperation and immediacy filled Pierre. "Let's do it!" he chuffed. Pierre and Drago bumped chests in the way that male-dogs do; then they sprinted over to the sand trap. Cappy stood dogwatch on the grassy ridge above the site, and cried, "Dig in!"

The dogs sprang forward, plowing their paws into the desert sand, like 49ers shoveling for California gold. Sand blew and flew all over the place as they dug in frenzied delight. Cappy could barely make out the canine forms beneath the sandy blur and jumping fur. And so it continued into the night, with thoughts of great treasure igniting the site!

As the moon hastened towards the horizon, our treasure hunters grew weary. Frequent trips to the water hazard revived flagging spirits, but Doglantis was becoming a distant, perhaps unattainable dream. As Doom, and his best friend, Gloom were about to envelop the group, Olivia dug up a basket about the size of a sack of kibble. As she was brushing it off with her paw, Drago and Summer unearthed a long, flexible, wooden pole. Pierre discovered a trove of arrowheads. Each and every dog found something of interest. There were baskets of various shapes with designs of rattlesnakes, eagles, and lightning bolts woven into them. There were buckets of acorns, and sandals made of palm fronds. There were squirrel skeletons and bone awls. There were scraps of worn deerskin, everything but the Doglantis treasure.

Pierre voiced their shock and disappointment: "What do we make of this? Where are the treats, the toys unimaginable? What should we do? Dig deeper?"

Cooper stepped forward, and pawing at the sand declared, "Nothing here resembles any Poochasaurus artifacts I've ever heard of. We may have stumbled onto remnants of an indigenous population, maybe a local tribe…" "Do we take the stuff home or not?" asked Drago gruffly. Impatience, confusion, and fatigue gripped the group. As they jumped about and argued amongst themselves, a mysterious black van rolled silently onto the green. A great big bear of a man jumped out, "What in dog nation is going on around here?" he bellowed. The treasure hunters froze in their tracks.

Chapter 6

· · · · · · · · · · · · · · · · · · · ·

Luckily, quick-thinking Pierre signaled to Drago and said, "You and your pals take Cappy back to his cousin's house. I'd feel terrible if he got into trouble because of us." Drago and company whisked Cappy into the darkness of the golf course, away from what looked like a messy situation at the 18th hole. Pierre, Cooper, Summer and Olivia stayed behind to deal with the big man from the black van.

He grabbed a flashlight from his vehicle, and began sorting through everything the dogs had excavated. "I gotta say, you hounds may have actually uncovered some things of archeological value here. Why you did it, and what you planned to do with it are head scratchers. But for now, I'm gonna tape off the area, and get you back home. The sun is just now rising, and something tells me that your owners are going to be missing you. I shudder to think how that golf cart got here, but for the time being, I'll tag it and leave it at the site…"

"As I check your tags, you four trouble makers, hop in the van and we'll get on the road." Heads hung lower than low, they crept into the back of the van, each considering how the adventure of a lifetime morphed into a tale of disappointment and woe. The dogs were returned to their homes, dirty and disheveled. In the doghouse does not even begin to describe the trouble these friends were in.

Pierre got a thorough scrubbing, and a lengthy verbal drubbing. From Kathy's conversations with Isobel, Karen and Denise it sounded like his buddies received similar treatment. Kathy told him to go lie down and stay out of trouble. No treasure, no treats, no toys, no fun. The forlorn poodle prince settled in for a nap.

Sometime in the afternoon, Kathy got a call from the manager of the Duffer Valley Golf Club, requesting that she and Pierre come to the club by 4:00 p.m. The same request was made of Cooper, Summer, Olivia and their owners. Kathy feared that the manager would demand payment for the damage to the sand trap on the 18th hole. She looked at Pierre with profound disappointment, and he withered under her gaze. Causing such distress was never part of the Doglantis plan.

They arrived at the clubhouse and the dogs and owners were ushered into a spacious lobby. "Everyone take a seat, my name is Jim Wright, and I am the manager of Duffer Valley. We have a situation here that needs addressing," he said with a sly grin.

"We'll start with a brief explanation of what happened last night on the 18th hole by our chief of security Max Griffin." Max stood, and looking steadily at the four curious pups, began: "Twelve years of security work did not prepare me for the incident I drove into last night – a crew of canines covered in sand, a sand trap under siege, and all kinds of items strewn about that had been uncovered by the dogs."

"Many of the culprits ran off when I arrived, but these four stayed behind, seemingly to face the consequences of their undertaking. After I delivered the dogs to their homes, I called the manager. We felt that the unearthed items were likely of historical, indigenous value, so we got in touch with the leaders of the Cahuilla Tribe of California Indians, hoping they could make sense of the dig site."

The manager cut in, "Thanks Max. We have representatives here from the Agua Caliente, and Los Coyotes bands, members of the larger ancestral Cahuilla Tribe. Ed, would you like to speak on behalf of the Tribal Council?"

"Yes. Thank you all for coming. We got the call this morning about baskets, arrowheads, awls and other utensils that were dug up right here. Of course, our interest was piqued. While having dogs run amok all night isn't a good idea, we have to admit, all's well that ends well. Though we may never know what inspired your dogs to meet up for a big dig at the sand trap, they did the Cahuilla Tribe and the City of Palm Springs a great service."

"You may know that the Cahuilla peoples settled here some 2,500 to 2,000 years ago. Your dogs unearthed several items of a village that is at least a thousand years old. While there is much more excavating to do, we are grateful to Duffer Valley for preserving this site. It will be cordoned off, and eventually a replica of the authentic village will be erected there. If you are a golfer, fear not: the 18th hole will be rerouted to accommodate this native treasure. The village will be open to the public and will hopefully encourage locals and tourists alike to delve into the rich culture and history of our ancestors."

"Call it serendipity or divine humor, but Mukat, the Creator in our mythology, appointed the dog as protector of his people. In ancient times, dogs played an indispensable role, protecting our homes from bears, cougars and other predators. Today, we are grateful to these four dogs for uncovering so many of our artifacts intact, sparking renewed interest in our history and culture. Dogs acting as loyal friends, yet again. Well done!"

"Please bring Pierre, Cooper, Summer, and Olivia up to the front so we can give them their medallions engraved with their names in English and Cahuilla. They will also receive a year's supply of treats, and a native, lightning bolt basket filled with all kinds of toys, donated by Canines-R-Us. The dogs all caught the words "treats" and "toys". Tails started to wag with abandon, and cries of excitement interrupted the man's speech.

As they brought the honorees forward, the owners were dumbfounded and profoundly proud of their pooches. No one could have guessed the day would end this way.

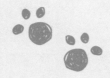

Epilogue

· · · · · · · · · · · · · · · · · · · ·

(Tail End)

That night, Dog Park 3 was abuzz with the amazing news of the day. Dogs from near and far parks came to high-five the heroes who brought such honor to all of dogdom. As the place cleared out, Pierre, Cooper, Summer, and Olivia settled on a grassy patch under the Acacia tree's lovely umbrella.

Pierre slid down onto his tummy, at ease and yet curiously spring-loaded. He quipped, "Well we may not have discovered the Lost Isle of Doglantis, but we surely came away with great treasure!" "Well done," said Cooper who closed his eyes for a quick snooze. "I wonder if we'll ever see Drago again…" mused Summer. Olivia, flat on her back with paws akimbo, and head rocking back and forth, cried merrily, "I can't wait to get back in the golf cart again!"

That very August night, the Perseids were creating their own celebration over Dog Park 3 and the entire planet, with a meteor shower of unparalleled beauty. It could be said that all was right in the universe that night.

Printed in the United States
by Baker & Taylor Publisher Services